William Scaling

The Salix or Willow

Part 2

Anatiposi

William Scaling

The Salix or Willow

Part 2

Reprint of the original, first published in 1872.

1st Edition 2023 | ISBN: 978-3-38218-956-3

Anatiposi Verlag is an imprint of Outlook Verlagsgesellschaft mbH.

Verlag (Publisher): Outlook Verlag GmbH, Zeilweg 44, 60439 Frankfurt, Deutschland
Vertretungsberechtigt (Authorized to represent): E. Roepke, Zeilweg 44, 60439 Frankfurt, Deutschland
Druck (Print): Books on Demand GmbH, In de Tarpen 42, 22848 Norderstedt, Deutschland

THE

SALIX OR WILLOW:

IN A SERIES OF PAPERS,

BY

WILLIAM SCALING,

Ten Years Basket Maker to Her Majesty and the Royal Family.

PART II.

HISTORY, CLASSIFICATION, ETC.

"We pass a gulf in which the willows dip
Their pendant boughs, stooping as if to drink."—COWPER.

LONDON:

SIMPKIN, MARSHALL, AND CO., STATIONERS' HALL COURT.

NOTTINGHAM: R. B. EARP, MARKET STREET, LONG ROW.

1872.

SALIX OR WILLOW.

PART II.

Historically considered the willow is an object of considerable interest. One of the first occupations of uncivilized man has been the weaving of twigs into various articles of use or ornament, and willows being indigenous to nearly every part of the world, it is presumable they would be employed for that purpose in preference to any other plant. We are told the Ancient Britons were so clever and expert in the manufacture of useful and ornamental baskets that a considerable quantity of baskets (Bascandoe) of their make were sent to Rome, and there realized high prices. Their huts, boats, shields, and other articles were also constructed of wicker work; and even so late as the Anglo-Saxon period, in Wales, the chief palace of the King, and place of assembly for the great council of the nation was called the white palace, from the osiers of which it was constructed being peeled; and we learn from the *Leyes Wallicea* that a fine of one pound and eighty pence shall be paid by whoever shall burn the King's hall or palace. Eight buildings or dependencies upon the palace (similarly constructed) are also named, the destruction of each of which is valued at one hundred and twenty pence. These buildings are the dormitory, the kitchen, the chapel, the granary, the bakehouse, the stable, the storehouse, and the dog house. The value of the palace of the Welsh King will be seen from the money of the period, the pound being equal to £2 16s. 3d., and the penny to 2¾d. of our present money. The discoveries of Layard in the ruins of Nimroud prove that the twigs of willow were used at that early date in the manufacture of baskets, and he speaks of bridges of basket work in the Tiyari Mountains sufficiently strong for animals and men to cross.—Page 136 of " Nineveh." The allusions in Holy Writ to willows and baskets are numerous. " By the rivers of Babylon, there we sat down, yea, we wept when we remembered Zion; we hanged our harps upon the willows iu the midst thereof." Sir Thomas Dick Lauder remarks that the tender and melancholy recollections of the children of Israel, when taken in conjunction with this tree, are in themselves sufficient to give it an interest in every human bosom. Herodotus alludes to the willow divining rods of the ancient Scythians. The branches of a weeping willow on the Euphrates are said to have caught the crown from the head of Alexander the Great, as he passed under the tree in a boat, which circumstance made the diviners predict his doom. Pliny mentions eight different sorts of willows, and he speaks of the willow as one of the most useful acquatic trees; and according to Cato, in the days of ancient Rome a crop of willows was considered next in value to the vineyard and the garden, and he enumerates the many uses the willow is put to. At Lanark, according to ancient usage, the boys of the Grammar School parade the streets the day before Palm Sunday, carrying a willow tree in bloom, ornamented with spring flowers. See C. A. John's "Forest Trees of Britain," page 245. And in some parts of Yorkshire a similar custom prevails.

The earliest notice we have of the willow is in *Leviticus* xxiii. 40, where the Israelites are told to "take the boughs of goodly trees, branches of palm trees, and the boughs of thick trees, and willows of the brook, and to rejoice before the Lord their God seven days." The prophet *Isaiah* xliv. 4, speaking of the restoration of Israel, says "They shall spring up as among the grass, as the willows by the water courses." In the book of *Job*, xi. 22, where Behemoth is said to be "compassed about with willows of the brook; and again, *Ezekiel* xvii. 5, speaking of the last branch of the house of Judah, says that "A great eagle cropped off the topmost twig of a cedar tree, and set it by the waters as a willow tree." Bruckhardt speaks of a noted fountain in Syria, called Ain Saffat, or the Willow Fountain.

The greater number of willows are of the temperate and colder regions, yet they are spread over a wider range of the earth's surface than any other ligneous plant. Humboldt and Bonpland found it in South America, near the equator; Royle discovered several sorts which he describes as indigenous to India, both on the mountains and on the plains; Dr. Richardson, in the appendix to Franklin's first journey, speaks of the *Salix Arctica, Salix Rostrata,* and others, as growing on the extreme limit of vegetation. Captain Parry, in his journal of his voyages for the discovery of the North-West Passage, in speaking of the Esquimaux of Melville Peninsula, Winter Island, and Igloolik, tells us that for the purpose of obtaining fire the Esquimaux use two lumps of common iron pyrites, from which sparks are struck into a little leathern case, containing moss, well dried, and rubbed between the hands; if this tinder does not readily catch, a small quantity of the floss of the seed of the ground willow is laid above the moss, and as soon as a spark has caught, it is gently blown till the fire has spread an inch around, when the pointed end of a piece of oiled wick being applied, it bursts into a flame, the whole process having occupied perhaps two or three minutes. Dr. Lindley says the willow is the most northern woody plant known. Pursh describes several kinds indigenous to North America. The *Salix Babylonica* is a native of Armenia, and is also indigenous to China and Japan. The Cape of Good Hope, and also New Zealand have their native willows. In the dreary plains of Siberia, and on the Oural Mountains willows are found. The *Salix Devaricata* is found on the Alpes of Dauria, growing amongst granite rocks. Several other willows grow freely in strong desolate wastes, indeed the only kind of land the willow seems unable to grow in is peat bog. No ligneous plant will stand the extremes of climate, or bear removal from a warm to a cold situation, or *vice-versa,* so well as the willow. It will thrive under a tropical sun, or in the desolate ice-bound regions of the North, on the barren hill, or the fertile plain.

Sir W. J. Hooker observes that the many important uses rendered to man by the different species of willow or osier seem to rank them among the first in our list of economical plants. The bark and leaves of the willow are astringent, and the bark of most sorts of willow may be used for tanning, and it is a fact worth noticing, that the tanners of Norway and Russia use willow in preference to oak bark, and much of the excellence of Russian leather is said to be due to the use of willow bark. M. Lennox, a Frenchman, discovered a substance which he named " Salicine," in willows. It is in the form of greyish crystals, and extremely bitter.   M. Magendie says he has known three doses of six grains each stop a fever; and Professor Burnet says it is equally as efficient as Peruvian bark in cases of fever, and speaks of the wise provision of Providence in placing the remedy for agues and other low fevers in moist situations where those diseases are most prevalent. It is not quite certain which variety of willow produces " Salicine" in the greatest abundance, but it is most likely the *Salix Purpurea*, and its varieties, as being the bitterest willows, and it is a noteworthy fact that all the varieties of the bitter willow will grow in the wettest soils. Hasselquist, in his letters from the Levant, says the " Calaf" is a little willow which does not grow to a large tree ; it has a straight trunk, with a smooth oval lancet-shaped leaf, deeply sawed on the edges. No tree in Egypt is more famous among the inhabitants on account of the water that is distilled from its blossoms in spring, and which is much used by the Egyptians as a family medicine. They are scarcely afflicted with any disease but they use the waters of " Calaf." There are apothecaries in Cairo whose chief, almost only, employment is to sell " Calaf," for thus they likewise call the water. It is cooling, promotes perspiration, and is somewhat cordial. It therefore serves in the continual fevers which are so common in Egypt during the summer season. /

The flowers of the willow are eagerly sought by the honey bee, and coming earlier than the flowers of other trees, are especially valuable on this account. In Norway, Sweden, and Lapland the green shoots and leaves are collected, dried, and stored, for the use of cattle. The leaves and tender shoots of most of the sallows and of the *Salix Vimi-nalis* tribe are eagerly eaten by horses, cows, or sheep. Captain Parry states that the Esquimaux use the leaves of the willow as food. The seed down is used by certain birds to line their nests with. The wood of the willow is used by cork cutters for sharpening their knives, and by turners for polishing other woods when in the lathe. The wood of the willow is light, smooth, soft, and extremely tough; it will bear more hard knocks without splinter or injury than any known wood, and hence it is always used for making cricket bats. Whenever it can be obtained it is used for the floats of paddle steamers or the strouds of water wheels. It wears longer in water than any other wood. It is used as breaks for railway coal wagons and luggage trucks, and is the only wood that will stand that kind of pressure and concussion, without fracture. Its extreme elasticity and toughness constitute it the best of all material for the sides and bottoms of carts and barrows, when rough work, such as leading coal or stone is required, and were it obtainable in sufficient quantity, it would be the very best material for constructing the carriages for passenger traffic on our railways, since carriages made of this wood would be less liable to be broken into splinters by collisions. The wood of the willow burns slowly and is not easily set on fire, a quality which ought to be a considerable recommendation where it is necessary to use wood in close proximity to fire. Willow was always used by powder manufacturers for charcoal in preference to other woods, and was only discontinued because the supply fell short. The wood of the willow is much esteemed by painters for their crayons. The spray of the willow is manufactured into an almost endless variety of articles, both of use and ornament, by the basket maker, and is of sufficient importance to demand a special notice hereafter. According to Mr. F. G. Packer, the market gardeners in the immediate neighbourhood of London alone buy of the merchants 10,000 bundles of willow twigs annually, at the average value of 5s. per bundle, for tying up vegetables for the London markets, independently of what they grow themselves for the same purpose. The shoots of willows are also used for tying up the branches of trees to espaliers, &c. Large quantities of hoops for cooper's purposes are made of willow shoots of two or three year's growth, chiefly in Holland, and exported to various parts of the world. Rows of willows planted on the banks of streams or rivers are well adapted for preventing the encroachment of the water, the grasp and tenacity of their roots holding the bank together. Willow wood is cut up into fine strips or shavings for the ornamentation of grates when fires are not in use, and woven into sheets for the use of basket makers. Willow is also used for manufacturing articles, in imitation of ebony, as it readily takes the dye, and is susceptible of a high polish. To the toy maker and wood turner willow is valuable. As cutting boards for shoemakers and others willow is in demand. As a screen or nurse to young plantations in bleak or exposed situations, willow is the most useful plant we possess. For the game covert we have no plant so easily reared, and at the same time so effective and profitable. Our hedges might also be constructed of willows, with the advantage of being easily reared, forming a stronger and better shelter in winter, and paying the farmer for growing, instead of costing him a considerable amount to keep in repair, with no return, as our hawthorn hedges do at present.

As a nurse or shelter to other trees in exposed situations, the willow is one of the best trees known; its power to resist the force of storms is well understood; the lightness of its branches and foliage, together with its great elasticity, enables it to bend to the blast that would break or uproot the oak, ash, elm, or even the pine. Of the extreme hardiness of certain kinds of willow it is almost unnecessary here to speak. Sir J. W. Hooker says it is the most northerly ligneous plant known. One of the essentials in a nurse tree for young plantations is quickness of growth, and, with the exception of the poplar, no tree can compare with the willow in this respect. It may be said that the willow being deciduous, and of thin straggling formation, would not afford the necessary protection during the winter months, and that in summer protection is not required. To this it may be replied that few if any deciduous trees receive injury from the winter storms, and that no more protection is then needful than would be afforded by a few rows of leafless willows. The time when protection is essential is in the spring and early summer, and it is then the willow would be of the greatest service, for coming into leaf and flower earlier than any other forest tree, often covered with its silvery coat by the middle of February, in the north of England, and fully clothed by its coat of foliage by the end of March or early in April, it affords ample protection at the time protection is most needed. Referring to a register kept in the Basford Nursery in 1871, of nearly 300 varieties of willows 92 were in flower and 115 in leaf on the 25th of March. An effectual screen under the shelter of which the more tender forest trees could be reared is easily made by planting three or four rows of well-rooted willows three feet apart each way; and hardly any soil is so poor, or so exposed that such willows would not grow in. The value of such a screen will be well understood by the practical forest planter, for under its protection he would be enabled to convert many of our now bleak and desolate spots into remunerative forest land. In many cases large sums of money have been expended in trying to raise plantations, in exposed situations, with small success, the failure arising in most cases from the want of shelter or nurse trees sufficiently hardy to stand the exposure; and yet the willow, one of the hardest trees known, does not appear to have been thought of, except by a very limited number of planters.

As an ornamental tree probably none commands such universal admiration as the weeping willow, *Salix Babylonica*, with its long delicate pensile branches suspended over an ornamental lake, as the poet expresses it, " Stooping as if to drink." Jutting from a promontory, or hanging over sculptured marble like graceful drapery, it conveys to the mind a feeling of repose unmixed with gloom, and if we can imagine a tree to have expression, this may be said to express a feeling of peaceful rest. Throughout the East, including China, it is used in the burial places as a semblance of repose, than which no object could be more appropriate. As may be supposed, from its Eastern origin, the *Salix Babylonica* is somewhat tender, and in the North of England and Scotland requires the protection of other trees when planted in exposed situations. Proximity to water, however, is not essential to its perfect development, and in common with most other willows, it has great power of resisting drought. In landscape the weeping willow harmonises well with the Lombardy poplar, or other spiry topped trees, and in a judiciously-chosen site nothing can exceed it in grace and beauty, or be more gratifying to an artistic eye. The date of the introduction of this tree into England is a debated point, some ascribing it to Mr. Pope, and others to Mr. Vernon, a merchant of Aleppo, about the beginning of the last century; others say it was first planted at Kew, in the year 1692.

There are many other pendulous willows equally as beautiful as the

Salix Babylonica, although differing widely from it in appearance—*Salix Prunosea Pendula, Salix Japonica Pendula, Salix Cærulea Pendula,* and others, which in the course of this work it is intended to illustrate. Some of those now before the public budded or grafted upon standards, and looking like overgrown mushrooms, are very handsome when trained upon their own stems, with sufficient space to show their special peculiarities of growth. And I cannot but think that the custom of budding upon standards, and training into a mathematical precision of form any tree that possesses an artistic irregularity of itself, is much to be regretted, and is almost as offensive to a correct taste, as the clipping of our naturally handsome evergreens into a supposed resemblance of animals or objects not to be found in nature unadorned.

Of shrubby willows there are many worthy of a place in our ornamental gardens. *Salix Pentandra, Salix Lucida,* and one or two others have such a close resemblance to the laurels, as to be frequently mistaken for varieties of that plant. Others again have very dark corrugated foliage, seldom reaching more than seven to ten feet in height, and are of a close compact form, with very little of that straggling habit found in ordinary willows. We have also many dwarf varieties of extremely slow growth, one or two of them not rising over six or seven inches in as many years, with others that creep along the ground like fine threads, admirably adapted to plant in rockwork, and all those dwarf or shrubby varieties produce the well-known palm, which in the case of some of them, as *Salix Lanata,* will remain for several weeks without much apparent change, blooming in early spring when flowers of any kind are a great consideration.

Independently of the very considerable profit attending the growth of tree willows, some of them are of great beauty. The *Salix Alba,* when not mutilated by pollarding, is both a beautiful and cheerful looking object, with silvery tinted foliage, looking like a huge feather, sprinkled with silver. The *Salix Aura,* or golden willow, is also very handsome, and worthy of more notice than it has yet received, both as an ornamental and a timber tree. The *Salix Carteriana,* or red-twigged mountain willow, with its dark red branches and spiry head, is eminently calculated to add beauty to our woodlands. *Salix Regalis*, although not attaining to the size of some of the other tree willows, is one of the most silvery trees we have, and although it was introduced in the last century, it is hardly yet known to our nurserymen. *Salix Basfordiana* and *Salix Sanguinea*, two lately introduced varieties, are amongst the most beautiful deciduous forest trees we now possess, and all who have seen them have considered them entitled to occupy the first place as ornamental forest trees. They are spiry-topped trees, and their manner of growth similar to the well-known Bedford willow, *Salix Russelliana*. The branches of *Salix Basfordiana* are of a brilliant orange colour, tipped with red, and the branches of *Salix Sanguinea* of a clear vermillion colour, and in winter, when divested of foliage, with the sun shining upon them, are as bright as if varnished. They are both vigorous growers, and attain a large size, *Salix Basfordiana* being the most vigorous grower of the two. They are perfectly hardy and will thrive in very exposed situations. It is also worthy of remark that the dense smoke of a town does not materially interfere with the healthy growth of willows, thus by planting ornamental willows many of our smoky manufacturing towns might be much improved in appearance, when other trees would not live. This circumstance has been made use of to a great extent by the able manager of the public parks of Glasgow, Mr. McLellan, who by a liberal use of only a limited number of varieties of ornamental willows, arranged also so as to protect more tender plants, has succeeded in making the parks of Glasgow worthy of comparison with the parks of any town in Great Britain, notwithstanding the very unfavourable atmosphere and dense smoke of its numerous manufactories. It has frequently been stated in works on planting, that the willow does not harmonize well with other trees. I believe Gilpin was the first to make this statement, and nearly every succeeding writer has copied his remarks without proof or investigation, until it has become generally believed. The statement is just as far from the fact as that fixed, but equally erroneous idea, that willows will only grow in wet or swampy soil.

To grow willow trees in perfection they must be planted closely, say three feet apart each way, or 4,840 to the acre would not be too close for the first eight or nine years, when they might be thinned out to half that number. The thinnings would find a ready sale for general farm purposes. At the end of sixteen or twenty years they might be reduced to 1,210 trees, or six feet apart each way, which would generally afford ample space for their full development. The time to fell such a plantation must depend very much upon circumstances. No unvarying rule can be laid down, but it is better to cut too early than to allow them to stand too long; for, as before stated, when the willow has reached its best it speedily decays. Its duration may be said to range from thirty to fifty years; but whenever dead branches begin to show themselves there should be no delay in cutting down. In felling willows do not think of leaving a few selected trees in the hope of obtaining large timber, for after having been so crowded and then suddenly exposed they would almost invariably perish. If heavier timber is desired, plant more openly at the first.

I will now endeavour to arrive at an approximate value of an acre of such timber at its prime, say after having been planted forty years. There is plenty of evidence to show that it is not an uncommon thing for a willow tree at thirty years of age to yield forty-five feet of measurable timber, or at the rate of $1\frac{1}{2}$ cubic foot per annum. The experiments of the Duke of Bedford and others proved this to be the case. I will not, however, reckon upon such great results, and will further assume that 110 trees out of our 1,210 are worthless, being a much greater margin than would be probable, and that in forty years we only produce one-third of the above, or half a foot instead of a foot and a half per annum. We shall then have 1,100 trees, containing an average of twenty cubic feet each, or 22,000 feet, worth, at the lowest computation, 1s. per foot, or £1,100, the produce of an acre of such wood in forty years, leaving the two thinnings to cover the cost of labour, which would be more than sufficient for that purpose. This is no fanciful calculation, but one fully borne out by the experiments of men whose words cannot be doubted. It cannot, however, be too often repeated that the willow will not arrive at perfection in swampy, undrained land. Willows grow freely on the slopes or tops of exposed hills; indeed, there are few situations in which they will not grow, but in no place so badly as in water-logged land. For timber trees the *Salix Fragilis*, or some of its kindred varieties, of which there are not fewer than twenty or thirty under cultivation, should only be employed, some of the lately introduced varieties being not only vigorous growers but extremely beautiful. It must also be borne in mind that all willows grow more vigorously from cuttings than from rooted plants; and, therefore, rooted plants only should be employed when immediate effect is desired.

CLASSIFICATION.

Professor Koch appears to have been the only writer on the Salicacea who has had even a glimpse at any clear method of classification, and yet he failed to arrive at any adequate mode of definition, which failure may, to some extent, be accounted for by the circumstance that he had not the opportunity of observing them all growing, for any length of time, under his own observation. He had in many instances to judge of them from dried specimens or plants sent to him from a distance by various collectors, grown in various soils and situations, and collected at various times of the season; and as willows are so greatly altered in colour of twigs, size of leaves, period of inflorescence, and general appearance at different periods of their growth, there is no wonder that the learned botanist should have frequently been at fault. Nevertheless he clearly saw there was a possibility of reducing the complications the genus was involved in, and gave it as his opinion that the tendency that existed to multiply the species, only increased the difficulty of reducing them to a system. Added to this, the willow belongs to that order of plants having the male and female flowers on separate trees, and the marked difference that exists between the sexes in appearance as well as vigour of growth—the female in every case being of more vigorous growth than the male—still further tended to complicate the matter. Also the hybridity of the willow has long been a subject for discussion, and has not yet been definitely settled. See "Journal of Botany," vol. ix., page 225, article by the Rev. J. E. Leefe, M.A., F.L.S. This being the case, every collector who has found a willow possessing any peculiarity he has not been accustomed to see, has felt himself at liberty to consider it a newly-discovered species. Could this question of seedling willows and hybridity be determined, the ground would be cleared for the settlement of the species, and a more simplified classification. The vast number of the now called species might then be found to be what I believe them, only varieties. As a practical basket maker and worker of willows, my attention was early directed to the special peculiarities of each variety that came under my notice, and the requirements of my trade rendering it necessary I should have all the best and finest willows known, I became a grower of willows, in order to obtain what my trade demanded. The necessity for growing them became a hobby or pleasure, and I was thus led to collect every obtainable variety, and also to read up whatever had been written on the subject. It is well known to every observant basket maker, that from the habit of constant manipulation he can with accuracy determine one variety of willow from another, merely by the sense of feeling, even when peeled or divested of its bark, and with greater certainty than an ordinary botanist can by an examination of the growing plants; the hardness or pliability, irregularity or smoothness of the surface, the straight or wavy tendency, are unerring indications of the variety of willow he has under manipulation.

In order to show the absolute necessity of a new classification a few examples of the present confusion will suffice. In the Botanical Gardens at Brussels, and the department set apart for the especial use of the students, is a small but well-managed Salictum, and in which more care and diffidence has been shown in the naming of plants than in any similar place known to me. Where any doubt has existed as to the true name the authorites are given. For example, the common and now well-known *Americana Pendula* appears as *Salix Triandra*, after Linneus, and as *S. Concolor* after Vratt. *S. Rubra*, by Huds, is *S. Concolor* by Host, and *S. Purpurea Viminalis* by Wim. *S. Purpurea Silicia*, by Wim, is called *S. Germanibus Glabris* by Vratt.

S. Mirabilis, of Host, is *S. Stylaris* of Seriange. *S. Repens*, by Linneus, is *S. Argenta* of Smith. There is a sallow called *S. Lambertiana* by Smith, and *S. Viminalis* is called *S. Alba* by Linneus. But the most extraordinary mistakes in those gardens are in the class *S. Cinerea*. We have *S. Cinerea Caprea*, *S. Cinerea Viminalis*, and *S. Cinerea Nigricans*. Many other mistakes equally as absurd occur, whilst the gardens in this country are in no better condition. The *S. Russelliana* of Regent's Park is the *S. Monandra* of Woburn, and *S. Mutabilis* of Edinburgh. *S. Aura* of Regents Park is the *S. Vitelliana* of Kew. Examples of this kind might be multiplied to an almost indefinite extent, but enough has been said to prove the necessity for some more simple and comprehensive classification. There is hardly a plant in my collection that has not been received under two or three different names. From the very excellent little work "Our Woodlands," published by Routledge in 1865, the following remark on the willow is extracted. "The study and classification of this extensive genus involves difficulties which have puzzled not only the tyro in botany, but even the accomplished professor of the science, who finds himself at a loss when trying only to determine the number of really distinct species. He may have before him the produce of a single botanical excursion—out of the group he will select several forms which correspond with what he has been accustomed to recognise as so many decided species; but this done, he will find remaining a number of doubtful forms intermediate between his so-called species, and which he can ascribe to neither, the leaves perhaps approach to those of one species, while the catkins or flowers are those of another, and the complication is increased by the fact that the willows belong to that section of trees that have the male and female flowers on separate plants, so that at last the perplexed botanist, finding that the willows refuse to be woven into his system, gives up the point and resigns the subject to the laborious plodding German mind, to which the very intricacy of the study serves as a charm and a stimulus." We have seen how far the German mind has accomplished this object by the list given in the Botanical Gardens of Brussels. The labour given to the subject no doubt has been great, but the result anything but clear or satisfactory. Another reason to be given why it has been found so difficult to classify the species, is the very great variation in the same plant at different periods of the year, or between a young plant and an old one. To give one example out of many. The flower and leaf of *S. Borreriana* and *S. Undulata* in the spring are identical in every respect; examine the two again when the flower has shed and the leaves well set, and you will find the leaf of *S. Undulata* to be wavy or undulated, whilst the leaf of *S. Borreriana* is perfectly flat. Other and unmistakable differences exist even in spring, but the above only shows how easily mistakes may be made when depending upon our present method of classification. It has been observed by Desfontaines that willows taken from the Alps and planted into gardens, so completely change their character and aspect, as not to be recognisable for the same species. In the Arboretum and Fructicetum of Loudon it is freely admitted that the inflorescence of the genus Salix is so great that it cannot alone be depended upon. Nor, I will add, is the rule of naming them from colour any more certain method, as in *S. Rubra*, red willow, *S. Cinerea*, grey or ash coloured willow, *S. Aura*, golden coloured willow, *S. Nigra*, black coloured willow, *S. Purpurea*, or purple coloured willow. Those colours are so changed by soil and situation as frequently to be mistaken for other plants by an ordinary observer. Some again have been named from certain peculiarities supposed to be possessed only by them. Thus *S. Corriacea*, leathery willow, and singularly as it may appear this is by no means a tough, pliable, or leathery willow. *S. Fragilis*, fragile willow, from the brittleness of its twigs. The twigs are certainly brittle when bent towards the tree, but this property is possessed in a still greater degree by the whole of the class amygdaliana or almond-leaved willow, of which there are thirty to forty varieties. *S. Viminalis*, so called from *vimen*, a twig or twiggy willow. But it is somewhat singular that this is one of the least twiggy willows we possess, nearly always growing with a straight, clear stem totally devoid of twigs. *S. Caprea*, or goat willow, so named in consequence of that animal being fond of browsing upon the leaves and flowers of this species of willow. It might be presumed from this that the goat preferred this willow to any other, which is not the case, for not only the goat but all browsing animals much prefer the flowers and leaves of S. *Viminalis* to any other variety of willow; and this confusion exists in every collection I have examined, and in every work that has been published on this subject, and as no two writers can agree in their classification, whilst probably few if any had the opportunity of observing them all in one trial ground for the same length of time, I venture to hope I may not be considered presumptuous in thinking that certain understandable rules may be laid down by which an ordinary observer may assign to them their proper position. I approach this subject with the full knowledge that I am laying myself open to the most severe criticism, but in extenuation it may be urged that all writers of any eminence on the genus Salix have admitted the confusion which exists; whilst Professor Koch and others have enforced the necessity of some one taking up this subject from the beginning, and thereby working up from a new standpoint, entirely disregarding what has gone before. It may be remembered that many botanists have considerable doubts respecting the existence of seedling willows, to any extent, and hence the tendency to multiply species in order to account for the very large number of divergencies. If we do not admit the hybridity of the willow, I do not see how we are to account for the unlimited number of varieties, and their very fine and almost imperceptible distinctions; the difference, in many cases, being so small, that unless they were grown upon the same plot of land, and under precisely similar conditions, it would be impossible to say any difference existed. Take as an example the *Salix Viminalis* or *Osier*: I have under cultivation in the same trial grounds, at present, not fewer than forty varieties; the so-called true *Salix Viminalis* has been sent. to me from many different gardens, yet hardly any two of them are alike. Some of them closely resemble each other; whilst others again, in vigour of growth, colour of bark, toughness of wood, &c., are widely dissimilar. One or two will make shoots from 14 to 16 feet in one season; yet others, under equally favourable conditions will not make more than 5 or 6 feet shoots in the same time. Some of them are extremely tough; others quite as remarkable for their tenderness; yet there can be no doubt of their all being one species. Take again the willow proper, or *Salix Fragilis*, and its numerous varieties; of this species I have nearly thirty under culture, varying widely in colour of stem and vigour of growth. Of *Salix Amygdaliana*, or Spaniard, as it is called by basket makers, I have between thirty and forty varieties, many of them varying widely in appearance, yet all well known to the trade by the peculiarity of their growth and solidity of their wood. The group or species called *Salix Purpurea* and *Salix Caprea* are equally prolific in the number of varieties, and yet, if we do not admit the fact of seedling willows, this very great number of varieties cannot be accounted for. That willows do not grow readily from seed under ordinary conditions must be admitted. Seed falling on the open ground, and exposed to sun and wind, will not grow; and even when sown in prepared beds, and with all the care and attention ordinarily bestowed upon seed beds, will generally result in failure; but they readily grow when they fall on friable soils that are well shaded from wind and sun, as in closely timbered plantations. In such places I have found hundreds of seedling willows in the space of a few square yards, and frequently many varieties in the same patch. In November, 1871, I found such a patch of 2 years old seedlings in a plantation of *Salix Kerksii* that had been left for three years old cuttings, and amongst these seedlings were varieties of *Salix Viminalis, Salix Amygdaliana, Salix Fragilis, Salix Caprea* and *Salix Kerksii*. I also found in the same month many hundreds one year old seedlings, in some places so closely set as almost to cover the ground, and containing many forms of willows. Many of those seedlings have been distributed to various persons, besides which, I had some hundreds potted for future examination. Several years ago I preserved some seedling willows, and carefully tended them; one of those, a species of *Salix Amygdaliana*, I now cultivate for basket making purposes, under the name of *Salix Germanica Alba*; it is a very distinct variety, and a most excellent basket willow. Many years ago I obtained, when on a ramble through the Ardennes, a very distinct variety of willow, known there as the red willow. At the time, it appeared to me the most handsome specimen I had met with, and well worth cultivating. I had a number of cuttings sent home and planted in the trial ground, and was pleased to find that in several kinds of soils it maintained its brilliant colour. In this trial ground there were between two and three hundred varieties of willows, and some three years' afterwards I was delighted to find several seedlings spring up which were duly preserved. One of those seedlings I now grow under the name of *S. Basfordiana*; and it has developed properties which entitle it to be considered one of the most handsome, deciduous trees, to be found in the country; it is the most vigorous growing tree willow I know. Planted side by side with the well-known *S. Russelliana* or Bedford willow, in five years, from cuttings, the proportions of each are as follow :—*S. Russelliana*, height, **15** feet, circumference of stem within four inches of the ground, 11½ inches. *S. Basfordiana*, height, **18** feet, and circumference, 13½ inches; it is a spiry topped tree, of the class known as *S. Fragilis*, and occupying but a small space to grow in. Its chief beauty, however, consists in the brilliancy of its colour. The branches are a brilliant orange, deepening into vermillion towards the tips, and when destitute of leaves in winter it shines in the sun as if varnished, and forms a very conspicuous and beautiful object when compared with our ordinary deciduous forest trees. The wood is extremely tough, more so than the Bedford willow, and the timber must be greatly sought after as soon as it can be got into the market, for cricket bats and other similar purposes. In the next number of this work it is intended to give an illustration of this tree *in colours*, from a photograph. To resume, I have under cultivation a seedling variety of *S. Triandra*, a very distinct sort, and also an excellent willow for basket making purposes, besides several others, the properties of which are not determined. I hope, also, to be favoured by reports from the several gentlemen to whom seedlings have been sent, which will, I doubt not, tend to set this question at rest. Being assured, however, that the greater number of willows we now possess are only seedling varieties, and not distinct species, the ground is considerably cleared for a new and more simplified classification. It appears to me essential that the generic name of each species should convey as clear an idea of its meaning as possible. The names of varieties may be arbitrary; but the name of each species should, if possible, give an idea of its general characteristics Feeling, as I do, all the responsibility of the work undertaken, it may not be out of place to give here an outline of the plan adopted to arrive at my present conclusions. The impossibility of making the genus conform to any existing system induced me to grow all the obtainable sorts in one trial ground, and it has thus turned out that plants received under different names, and of marked difference at first, have under such conditions proved to be identical. Assuming then, that nothing was known to begin with, a register has been kept in which every circumstance was recorded: as the size, shape and colour of bud; time of inflorescence; peculiarities of inflorescence; size and shape of stipules, or absence of stipules; time of coming into leaf, with size, shape, and colour of leaves; whether smooth, corrugated, or pubescent; colour of bark; deciduous duration of leaves; toughness of wood or twigs; specific gravity; method of growth and general configuration of tree; insects peculiar to each, &c., &c. And in addition to this, a collection of leaves and twigs, for constant reference, in which were noted the colour of such leaves and twigs when dried, also the toughness and bitterness of the dried twigs. Following this method the whole genus Salix is found to divide itself into certain natural classes; as, for example, a certain number of willows are found to produce their flowers before any sign of leaf is seen; another class is in full leaf before there is any appearance of inflorescence; another section has broad, corrugated leaves; others, again, smooth or glabrous leaves of a lanceolate form. These are broad distinctions, and may fairly be considered indicative of distinct species. It is only when the point is reached at which they appear to merge into, or combine the characteristics of any two species, that any difficulty occurs. However, as this might lead into the mist of speculation, I will leave it for the present, and confine myself to such points as may lead to a classification that can be understood. As this work is intended for the use of the general public, as well as the botanist, scientific terms will be as sparingly used as possible, consistent with clearness of description.

GROUP 1.—PURPUREA, OR THE PURPLE WILLOW.—This name, for reasons before stated, is not applicable to the group, inasmuch as the colour is not only altered by soils and situation, but the same colour is found in willows belonging to entirely different groups, and although such connot be said to be a distinguishing feature of this class, I do not propose to alter the specific name of any particular willow, but merely to group them under such heads, and by such names, as would not be applicable to any other group, and therefore unmistakeable; also, as far as possible, the system of minutely describing varieties when no real distinctions exist, will not be followed; for believing as I do that the great number of willows we possess are only varieties, and not species, such a system would only be of use to swell the dimensions of this book, without being of any profit to the reader. The following may be given as applicable to the group Purpurea :— Catkins coming early, before the leaves, and very compact; filaments 1; bearing anthers of 4 lobes *which are red before they burst*, and very conspicuous; germen sessile; scale of the bud black or partially so before shedding; upon the young branches of old trees leaves mostly opposite as in figure 2; obovate or widest towards the upper end as in figure 3; and nearly linear; smooth on both sides, with no perceptible corrugation; when young the leaves have, under all situations, a blue tinge; very smooth; very slightly serrated, chiefly toward the apex; in some of the varieties so slightly as only to be seen with a glass, and this serration does not show until the leaf is fully developed; the leaves and twigs all turn black in drying; the inner bark is yellow and intensely bitter, and the plant is never browsed upon by cattle, or eaten by rats or rabbits, except when under extreme pressure for food; footstalks of leaves extremely short, see figure 3; gland small; the bark in most of the varieties is striped longitudinally, especially near the root, which gives the stem a somewhat brindled or grey appearance; the twigs are very long, slender, and pliable, and have a wavy appearance. This in some of the varieties is more conspicuous than in others, yet to some extent they are all slightly wavy. When stripped of the bark the twigs are slightly corrugated towards the points, and the wood is yellow, or of a deep crimson colour, but if cut in winter, and boiled in hot water untill the peel can be removed, the wood is perfectly white, and the peel separates more easily from the wood than in any other class of willow. This property of peeling white when boiled makes it more valuable to the basket maker. as all other willows peel brown or foxy when boiled. Branches mostly spreading, wavy, or decumbent, with a flame-like motion in the wind; twigs when cut off the tree very tough and pliable; some of the varieties, as the *Americana Pendula*, with extremely fine pendulous twigs; these are generally budded on stocks, and sold as the American willow, whilst the *Salix Helix* is of upright growth, and very rigid; yet all, whether pendulous or upright, answer to the above description. Each group or species of willow may also be easily recognised by its habit of growth and general configuration; but as it would be impossible to convey these peculiarities to the mind of the reader without illustrations, photographs have been taken of living specimens of each group when destitute of leaves, in order to show their clear outline, and the leaves, twigs, and buds are shown of natural form. The size of leaves, twigs, and buds vary considerably in the several varieties, in consequence of favourable or unfavourable soils or situations, and whether old or young trees; young trees having in every case larger leaves than old ones, even when planted in the same ground; so that size alone is not to be relied upon, whilst the form never varies.

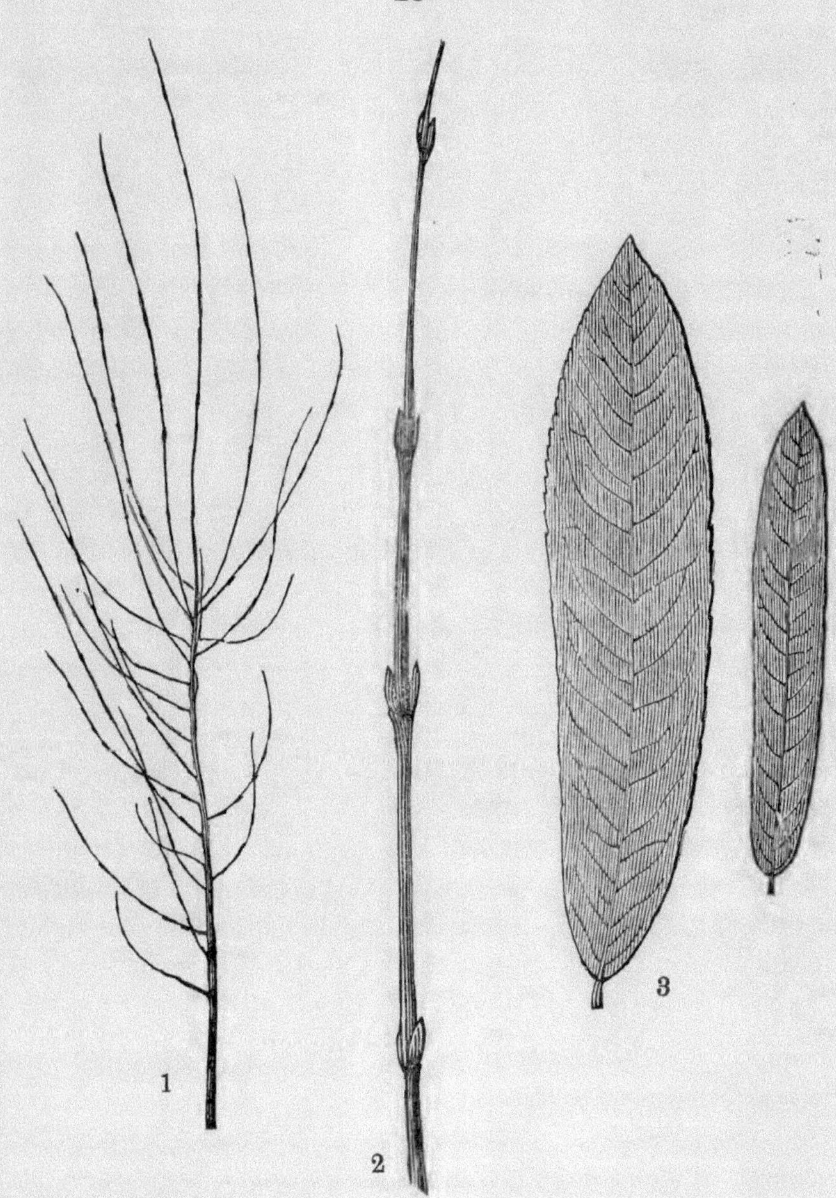

Fig. 1 is from a photograph of a young tree of this class, showing the wavy appearance of the branches peculiar to this group.

Special characteristics of female—ovary ovate, pubescent, sessile, stigmas divided and nearly sessile.—The one *special* distinguishing feature of this group, and one not found in any other, is having its *leaves opposite*, not invariably so, but nearly always upon the young twigs from old branches, and as this is *not the case* with any other member of the willow family, I shall call this group SALIX OPPOSITIFOLIO. The group includes *Salix Purpurea*, a low growing tree not reaching more than twenty to twenty-five feet in height, if left to grow its full size, producing long slender branches, wavy or decumbent.

Salix Lambertiana, a low growing tree, reaching a height of twenty-five to twenty-seven feet, branches a little thicker than *Purpurea*.

Salix Kerksii, a more vigorous plant, which does not attain to the dimensions of a forest tree, but much like the former *in growth and appearance*.

Salix Helix, a low shrubby tree, with branches more erect, and seldom attaining to a height of more than 14 or 16 feet, and the least suitable of any of the group as a basket willow, twigs hard and rather brittle. This is the plant which Loudon and others call the rose willow, from the peculiar bunch of leaves resembling a rose, produced by the bite of an insect. I have examined many thousand plants of this species but never yet found the rose upon it. The rose is frequently found upon the *Salix Fragilis*, *Salix Huntingdonia* and their varieties, and occasionally a very imperfectly formed one upon the *Salix Amygdaliana*. I cannot say it has never been met with upon *Salix Helix* but I have never seen it, and entertain considerable doubt of any one else having done so.

Salix Lanceolata. There is hardly any perceptible difference between this plant and *Salix Purpurea*.

Salix Mutabilis and *Salix Monandra*, as far as I can see, are strictly identical. I prefer to call it *Salix Mutabilis* on account of the many changes of colour the foliage undergoes in the course of its developement. It is a vigorous plant and grows more erect than any one of the group, but does not attain to the dignity of a tree.

Salix Wolgeriana. A more sturdy, compact growing tree, branches not so slender, leaves larger, but does not attain a greater height than the others.

Salix Forbyana, a large, strong ,growing plant ; which will when cut often send out shoots 10 to 12 feet long in one season, but not of much use as a basket willow, it is too coarse in its fibre ; will grow to a height of 35 to 40 feet.

Salix Americana Pendula. This is a well-known plant commonly used for budding upon stocks as a weeper. It is one of the smallest of the class, and in its natural state creeping over rocky ground, is a beautiful object. Its twigs are not sufficiently tough for basket work, except when grown upon its own roots and cut every year.

Salix Rubra. This plant reaches the extreme verge of this order ; in its growth it somewhat resembles *Salix Viminalis* or *Osier*, growing with straight, smooth, erect stem ; it also attains a much greater elevation than any of the others. The leaves are not quite so clearly defined in shape as those previously named, being somewhat longer and more accuminate, but not pubescent, as all the group *Viminalis* are, but when closely examined the branches have the wavy appear ance before noted, some of the buds are found opposite—the great distinguishing feature in this group—the inner bark is yellow and bitter, the stripped twigs have the same kind of corrugations, the wood the same peculiarities in drying white when boiled, and yellow when not boiled ; the catkins coming before the leaves, and distinguished by the same marks. The leaves and bark dry black, and in every other respect the same description holds good ; and however the statement may be received, I am driven to the conclusion that *Salix Rubra* is a hybrid offspring between the *Salix Viminalis* and *Salix Purpurea.*

In the Basford nursery there are several varieties of the same group, which have been sent to me under distinctive names, but which when grown in the same trial ground are either identical, or so nearly so, with those above named, it would consequently only be a waste of time to notice them, the more so as I believe the varieties of each group to be extremely numerous, and therefore to make the attempt would only tend to complicate instead of simplify this unravelled botanical puzzle.